MARSHALL ARMSTRONG is NEW to OUR SCHOOL

David Mackintosh

HarperCollins *Children's Books*

Marshall Armstrong is new to our school.
Miss Wright says he should sit at the front of our class,
just for the first few days until he settles in.

He looks different to me.

Marshall Armstrong sits next to me.
His things are different to mine.

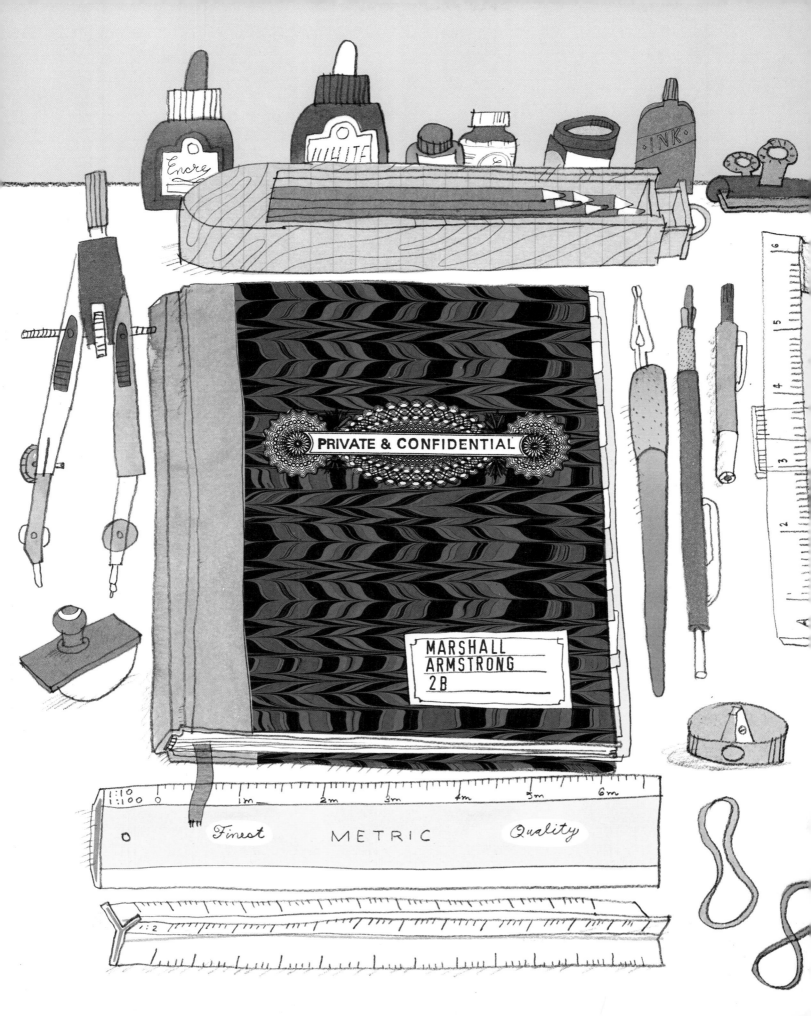

Marshall Armstrong's ear looks like a shell.

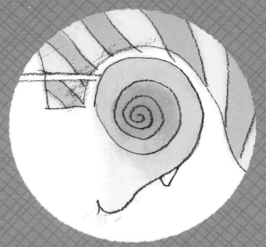

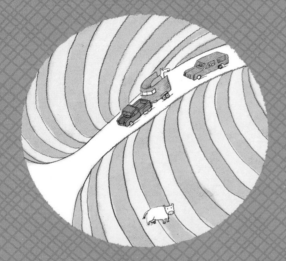

His hair reminds me of driving in the countryside to visit Gran.

He has pinched his glasses from another boy.

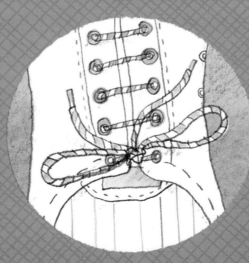

His laces are straight, not criss-crossed, like mine.

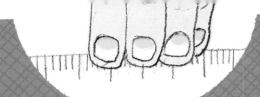

His freckles look like
birdseed on his nose.

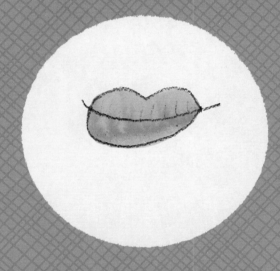

He has lips like my
tropical fish, Ninja.

And his eyes are always **looking at the front.**

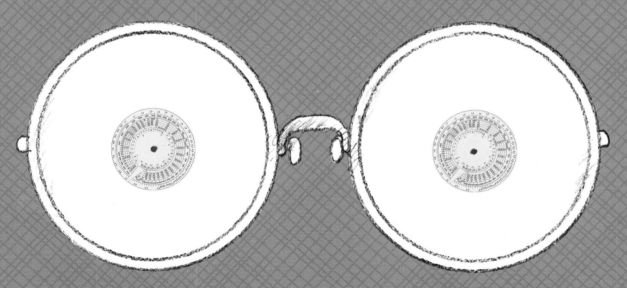

Marshall Armstrong's arm is too close to mine.

It is all white with red spots on it.

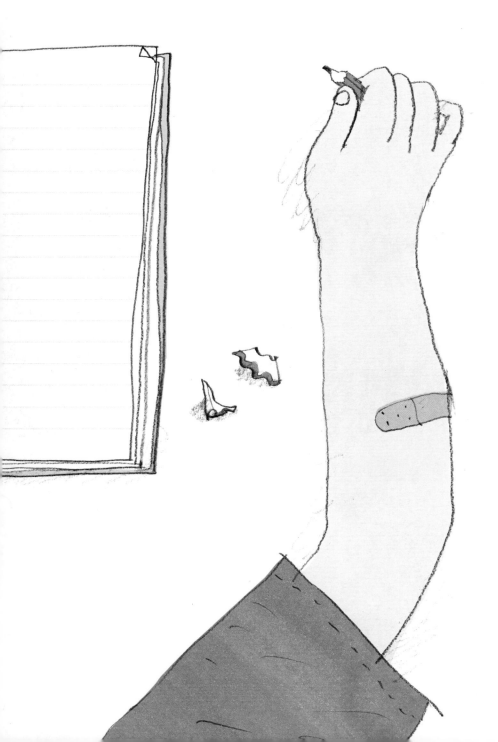

He says it's on account of mosquitoes liking him more than me.

His watch doesn't even have hands.

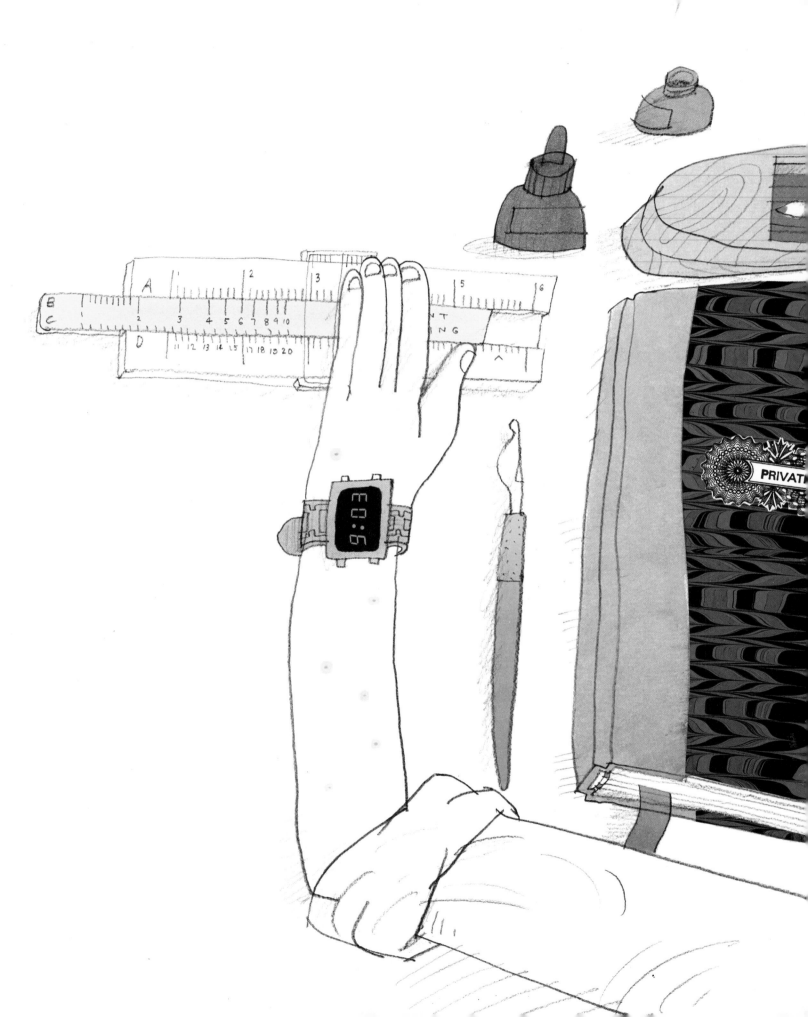

Marshall Armstrong doesn't eat normal food.
We call it space food, because it comes in silver wrappers.
Every wrapper has the name of the food inside it
written on the outside in black letters.

EGG, POACHED :2

CONSOMME, BEEF x1

ROAST CHICKEN & VEGETABLES :1

OTHER SIDE OPEN

DAY ONE : MEAL TWO

NO STEP

DOG, HOT x1

BAR, MUESLI x1

DESSERT, AMBROSIA x1

Then he has
a furry peach
for afters.

ACH

Marshall Armstrong can't participate in our Sports Day.
His doctor says that he should just sit with the
medicine balls and read his book.

Marshall Armstrong always wears a hat outside —
it's because of the ozone layer.

He tends to stay
in the shade.

Marshall Armstrong doesn't have a TV at home. He prefers the paper. His dad says it gives him a good perspective.

Marshall Armstrong doesn't fit in at our school.

Not one bit.

Marshall Armstrong has invited
everyone at school to his birthday party.
My mum says I have to go.

AND give him a present.

I'll probably have to sit next to him
the whole time, just like in school.

AND we won't be allowed to run about outside…

AND we won't eat fancy birthday cake
OR drink normal fizzy drink…

AND we'll all have to be careful
not to get too *hot and bothered*…

AND he'll make us read the
newspaper with his dad…

AND EVERYONE WILL
HAVE A TERRIBLE TIME.

Especially

ME.

BUT at
Marshall Armstrong's
house...

we can
run around
inside...

And...

Marshall Armstrong welcomes us playing Happy Birthday *on the piano he and his dad made.*

1, 2, 3, 4, 5, 6, 7, 8, 9, 10, 11, 12, 13, 14, 15, 16, 17, 18, 19, 20...

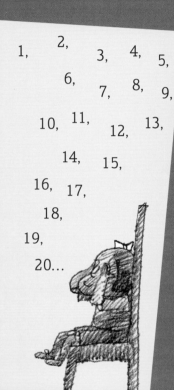

We rebuild Mr Armstrong's train set.

We all have a go at trying to light the bulb.

Geoffrey Feather wins Blind Man's Bluff twice, without looking.

We help put up Marshall Armstong's jungle tent.

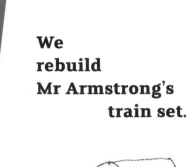

We have organic birthday cake, hot dogs and carrot cupcakes.

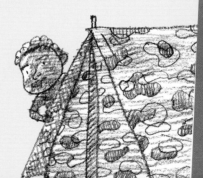

There is REAL lemonade made from lemons. And with pips.

There is a Mexican piñata to open.

We play hide-and-seek all over the house.

Bernadette has to go home early.

We swing on monkey bars.

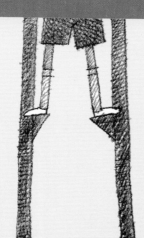

Marshall Armstrong completes the obstacle course in record time.

Then Mrs Armstrong lets us have a power nap.

We take turns to look at the sky through a telescope, and through a microscope at the cut on Jane's arm.

Marshall Armstrong performs on the piano he and his dad made, and he shows us a game with long, wooden sticks called cues.

OBSERVATORY ACCESS ONLY.

ENCYCLO
PAEDIA

Then,

we all have a ride down the special fireman's pole, from the top of the house to the bottom.

Mr Armstrong says that it's in case of emergencies, but you can also use it if you're in a hurry to answer the front door...

URSUS ARCTOS HORRIBILIS

or reach the toilet.

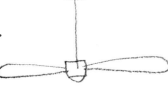

Before we leave the party, Marshall Armstrong's mother
gives each of us a party bag with our name on it.

I get Monster Gripping Paws, itching powder and
blood capsules. And a key ring with a light on it,
which I save for my mum.

HDAY

MARSHALL

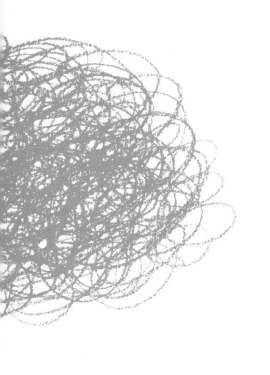

I tell her,

We had a GREAT time at Marshall Armstrong's party.

And Marshall is great too.

Elisabeth Bell is new to our school.
I tell Miss Wright that she should sit at the front
with me and Marshall for the first few days,
until she settles in.

RONGISNEW
EWTOOURSCH
STRONGISNEW
CHOOLMARSHA
SHALLARMSTIE
ISTRONGISNEW
EWTOOURSCH
OOLMARSHALL
ARMSTRONGIS
GISNEWTOOH

MARSHALL ARMSTRONG IS NEW TO OUR SCHOOL